Jack and the Beanstalk

Retold by Anna Milbourne

Illustrated by Lorena Alvarez

Jack and his mother were so poor, they never had enough to eat. One morning, they had nothing left at all.

"You'll have to take the cow to market and sell her," Jack's mother said sadly.

On the way, Jack met a strange little man.
"I'll give you these for your cow," said the little
man, holding out five wrinkly, dried beans.

"I need money, not beans," said Jack.

"Ah, but these are magic beans," said the little man.
"If you plant them, they'll grow into a
beanstalk so tall it touches the sky."

"Amazing!" said Jack. He gave his cow to the
little man, took the beans and ran off home.

But when he got home
he was in trouble...
big trouble...

"Jack, we need money,
not beans!" cried his
mother, and she threw the
beans out of the window.

Poor Jack went to bed hungrier and gloomier than ever.

What were they to do?

In the morning, even his room seemed gloomy.

His *room* seemed gloomy? Just a minute...

Outside his window was a giant beanstalk,
so tall it touched the sky.

"The little man was right!" thought Jack.
He scrambled onto the giant beanstalk
and climbed up... and up... and up...

...and there, at the top, he found a giant castle – with a giantess in front of it!

Jack gulped... Then his tummy rumbled.

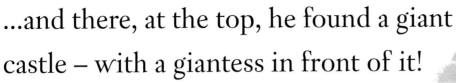

"Excuse me," he called out. "Please could you spare some breakfast?"

The giantess picked him up. "My husband munches and crunches little people like you," she said.

"I'll give you breakfast, but you'd better be gone before my husband gets home."

She whisked Jack inside, and set him down next to an enormous, crusty loaf. Breakfast had never tasted so good.

Mmmmm!

But then...

STOMP!

STOMP!

STOMP!

"Quickly, hide in here."
The giantess stuffed Jack
into a pot, just as a giant
strode into the kitchen.

Fee! Fi! Fo! Fum!
I smell the blood of an Englishman,
Be he alive, or be he dead,
I'll grind his bones to make my bread!

"Where is he?" demanded the giant,
and he started to search the table.

"You're imagining things," said his wife.
"Eat up your breakfast while I bring your hen."

She returned with the hen, and put it on the table.
"Lay!" commanded the giant.

Clink!

The bird laid a gleaming golden egg.

With a grunt, the giant closed his eyes and began to snore.

The giantess lifted Jack out of the pot.

"Run for your life!" she whispered.

But Jack had his eyes on the hen.

He grabbed the hen and fled for the door.
The bird let out a squawk!

...which woke the giant,
who saw Jack and let out a furious ROAR!

Jack dived out of the door and onto the beanstalk, with the giant hot on his heels.

Jack scrambled down the beanstalk
as fast as his legs would carry him.

"What's going on?" shrieked his mother from below. "Is that a– a– **GIANT?**"

"Just bring the axes!" Jack cried.

Jack and his mother chopped
and chopped at the beanstalk.

It creaked and it wobbled,
then it toppled over sideways.

The giant was flung
far over the hills.

They never
saw him again.

As for Jack and his mother, they lived happily ever after.

Each morning, the hen laid a golden egg, so they grew rich.
And Jack never climbed a beanstalk again.

About the story

Jack and the Beanstalk is an English fairy tale. The oldest known written version dates from 1807, but the story was around long before then. The cry "Fi, fo, and fum!" also appears in William Shakespeare's play, *King Lear*.

Taken from an adaptation by Susanna Davidson

Edited by Lesley Sims

Designed by Laura Nelson

First published in 2015 by Usborne Publishing Ltd., Usborne House, 83-85 Saffron Hill, London EC1N 8RT, England. www.usborne.com Copyright © 2015, 2014 Usborne Publishing Ltd.